THE GRUMPY PIRATE

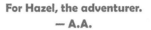

For our pirate crew: Devon and Morgan, Demetria and
Ariadne, Cyrus and Clay, Tegan and Garin, Max and Hazel, Ruby
and Theo, Sara and Sofia, and Julian, who are NEVER grumpy.
— C.D. and A.R.

For Hazel, the adventurer.
— A.A.

Text copyright © 2019 by Corinne Demas and Artemis Roehrig
Illustrations copyright © 2019 by Ashlyn Anstee

ISBN 978-1-338-60601-0

10 9 8 7 6 5 4 3 2 1   19 20 21 22 23

Printed in the U.S.A.   40
First printing 2019

Book design by Steve Ponzo

THE GRUMPY PIRATE

by **Corinne Demas** and **Artemis Roehrig**

illustrated by **Ashlyn Anstee**

Scholastic Inc.

Pirates aren't grumpy.
Pirates never pout.
Pirates smile and shout, "Aye aye!"
whenever they're about.

But there is one grumpy pirate.
They call him Grumpy Gus.

He grunts and gripes and grouses,
and always makes a fuss.

He will not eat his hardtack.
He will not drink his grog.

He glares out through the porthole
and grumbles at the fog.

The other pirates do their best
to help Gus try to smile.

He skips his shift to swab the deck.
He hates to coil the ropes.

Instead of helping trim the sails,
he mutters and he mopes.

The other pirates finally say,
"We all have heard enough!"

Gus moans,
"This ship's too tippy.
Our course is – **Aargh!** – too slow.

The deck is way too slippery.
I think I'll go below."

The pirates ask their queen for help.
"Grumpy Gus is such a crank.

Please save us from his grumpiness,
or have him walk the plank!"

The Pirate Queen (who is quite wise)
brings Gus a special friend.

"I'm giving you a parrot
to help your grumbling end."

Gus glowers at the parrot.
He asks, "What good are you?"

"What good are you?" the parrot asks,
and the parrot glowers, too.

The parrot follows Gus around
and echoes him all day.

He grumbles and he grouches in a very Gus-like way.

"I'm tired and I'm hungry.
I'm cold and I am hot.
I'm feeling very grumpy,
so I will frown a lot!"

Gus wails, "This parrot's crabby.
He's a sourpuss, a brat!
His voice is way too whiny.
Do I really sound like that?"

"Sorry, Gus," the wise queen says.
"The parrot sounds like you.
But if you change your attitude,
the parrot will change, too."

"I don't know if I can do it!"
Grumpy Gus begins to groan.

But then he hears himself and says,
"I'll try to change my tone."

Gus tries his
best at smiling.

The parrot tries
a beaky grin.

This makes Gus start to giggle.
And the pirates laugh with him.

"Mates, you've called me grumpy,
and I see," says Gus, "'twas true.
Now just call me Grinning Gus!"
"Aye aye!" shout all the crew.